You're a Brother, Little Bunny!

Maribeth Boelts

Illustrated by Kathy Parkinson

Albert Whitman & Company
Morton Grove, Illinois

Library of Congress Cataloging-in-Publication Data

Boelts, Maribeth, 1964–

You're a brother, Little Bunny! / by Maribeth Boelts; illustrated by Kathy Parkinson.

p. cm.

Summary: Life isn't quite the same for Little Bunny after baby Kale is born,

but he learns to love being a big brother.

ISBN: 0–8075–9446–6

[1. Rabbits — Fiction. 2. Babies — Fiction. 3. Brothers — Fiction.]

I. Parkinson, Kathy, ill. II. Title.

PZ7.B6338 Yo 2001 [E] — dc21 2001000804

The illustrations are rendered in watercolor and ink.

The display text of this book is set in Coronet Bold.

The text of this book is set in Pastonchi MT Regular.

Designed by Scott Piehl.

For more information about Albert Whitman & Company,

visit our web site at www.awhitmanco.com.

To Kathy Tucker, with my appreciation for
several years of patient and friendly editing.
M. B.

For Sabrina!
Welcome to the newest member of our family.
K. P.

When the first swirls of snow filled the sky, Mama gave Little Bunny a present. It was a boy baby doll, with a soft blue cap. "Now you can practice being a big brother," Papa said. "Your mama is going to have a baby."

Little Bunny was so excited he ran in and out of the house with questions.

"When will the baby be born? Will it be a boy baby or a girl baby? Can I take our baby for sharing time at preschool?"

Little Bunny practiced being a big brother all winter,

and he helped Mama and Papa get ready for the baby.

One morning, when the tips of tulips could be seen poking through the slushy snow, Mama and Papa went to the hospital. Grandma stayed with Little Bunny.

Later, the phone rang. "You have a brother!" Papa told Little Bunny. "His name is Kale."

The next day, Little Bunny met his brother.
"Gentle hands," Mama said.

Little Bunny touched his lips to the top of Baby Kale's head. "I love him," he said.

When Baby Kale came home from the hospital, Little Bunny changed his mind.

"If we didn't have a baby, Mama, I wouldn't have to plug my ears all the time."

"Babies do cry loudly," Mama said. "Would a walk outside with Papa help?"

There was a party to welcome Kale to the family.

"If we didn't have a baby, Papa, *I* would be getting presents,"
Little Bunny said.

Papa handed Little Bunny a silver box tied with ribbon.
"Unwrapping them for him is a big job to do."

A few nights later, Little Bunny sat on his bed. "If we didn't have a baby, Mama, you could sit by my bed and read me books and books and books!" he yelled.

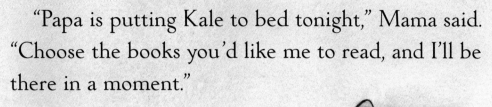

"Papa is putting Kale to bed tonight," Mama said. "Choose the books you'd like me to read, and I'll be there in a moment."

One morning, Little Bunny plugged his nose as Papa checked Kale's diaper. "If we didn't have a baby, then our house would smell good," he said.

Papa laughed. "I think your baby brother needs a bath, Little Bunny. Would you like to help me?"

Drizzle. Drizzle. Drizzle. The rain came down, and Little
Bunny was feeling restless. "If we didn't have a baby," Little Bunny
said, "I could stomp and bang a drum and growl like a monster
and not wake any baby up."

Mama gave Little Bunny an umbrella and opened the back door. "You stomp, bang, and growl all you want, and I'll watch."

At the grocery store, shoppers admired Baby Kale and told Little Bunny that he needed to be Mama's big helper.

"I don't want to be the big helper, Mama," Little Bunny said.
"That's okay," Mama said. "Just be our Little Bunny."

In the baby food aisle, Little Bunny chose carrots, peas, and peaches for Baby Kale. "Kale needs someone to taste these first, doesn't he, Mama?" Little Bunny asked.

"Of course," Mama said.

"I'm a good taster," said Little Bunny. "I'll taste the carrots when we get home."

Soon, it was Little Bunny's sharing day at preschool.

"The note from your teacher says that you may share something that begins with the letter *K*," Papa said, patting Kale's back to bring up a burp.

Little Bunny searched in his toy box. "I can't find anything that begins with *K*, Papa."

"Hmmm . . . let's keep thinking," Papa said as Kale squirmed. "Would you like to try burping him, Little Bunny?"

Little Bunny patted and rubbed Kale's back. Kale kicked his legs and let out a loud burp.

"If Kale could talk, he would say 'thank you,'" Papa said.

Little Bunny smiled and then made his silliest face ever. Kale watched and then made a sound no one had ever heard before.

"He laughed!" Little Bunny said. "I made Kale laugh!"

"You sure did!" said Papa. "It's his very first time."

Just then, Little Bunny had an idea. "Kale begins with *K*," he said. "I could bring my baby for sharing time!"

At preschool, Little Bunny showed his friends all the things that Baby Kale could do. "He can smile, and burp, and hold your finger, and . . . guess what else? He can laugh!"

That afternoon, Little Bunny helped Mama rock Baby Kale to sleep. "Mama?" Little Bunny said quietly. "If we didn't have a baby, then do you know what?"

"What?" Mama said.

Little Bunny snuggled close to drowsing Kale. "I wouldn't have . . . my brother."